Text copyright © 2010 by Cynthia Lord • Illustrations copyright © 2010 by Derek Anderson • All rights reserved. Published by Scholastic Press, an imprint of Scholastic Inc., *Publishers since 1920.* SCHOLASTIC, SCHOLASTIC PRESS, and associated logos are trademarks and/or registered trademarks of Scholastic Inc. No part of this publication may be reproduced, stored in a retrieval system, or transmitted in any form or by any means, electronic, mechanical, photocopying, recording, or otherwise, without written permission of the publisher. For information regarding permission, write to Scholastic Inc., Attention: Permissions Department, 557 Broadway, New York, NY 10012. • LIBRARY OF CONGRESS CATALOGING-IN-PUBLICATION DATA • Lord, Cynthia. Hot rod hamster/ by Cynthia Lord ; illustrated by Derek Anderson. — 1st ed. A hamster, with the help of a canine junkyard dealer and his mouse assistants, builds a hot rod and drives it in a race against some very large dogs. • ISBN: 978-0-545-03530-9 • [1. Automobiles—Fiction. 2. Automobile races—Fiction. 3. Hamsters—Fiction. 4. Dogs—Fiction. 5. Mice—Fiction.] I. Anderson, Derek, 1969-   ill. II. Title. PZ7.L87734Hot 2010 [E]—dc22 2009003930 12 11 10 9 8 7 6 5 4 3 2   10 11 12 13 14 • Printed in Singapore 46 • First edition, February 2010 • The display type was set in Ziggy ITC. • The text type was set in Cochin Bold, Gill Sans Bold. • The art for this book was done in acrylics. • Book design by Marijka Kostiw

To Abigail, Jessie, and Violet—C.L.

For Ron and Jane, who finally got
a hot rod of their own!—D.A.

Hot Rod Hamster

By
Cynthia Lord

Pictures by
Derek Anderson

Scholastic Press
New York

Old car, new car, shiny painted blue car,
Rust car, clean car, itty-bitty green car.

Which would *you* choose?

Smooth wheels, stud wheels, driving through the mud wheels,
Fat wheels, thin wheels, take her for a spin wheels.

Which would _you_ choose?

Coil parts, flat parts, gleaming this and that parts,
Round parts, straight parts, funny, out of date parts.

Which would *you* choose?

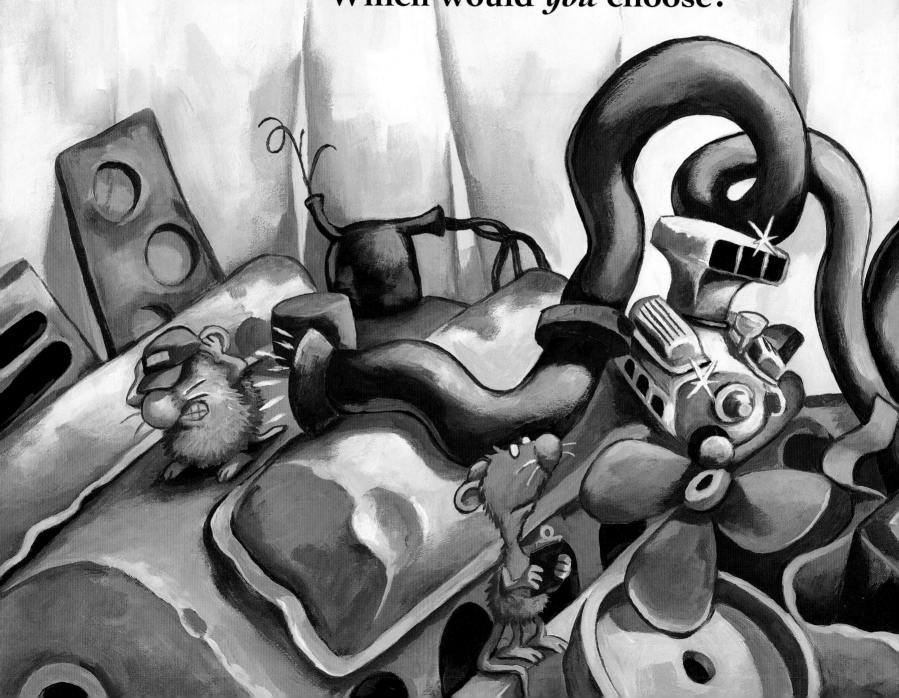

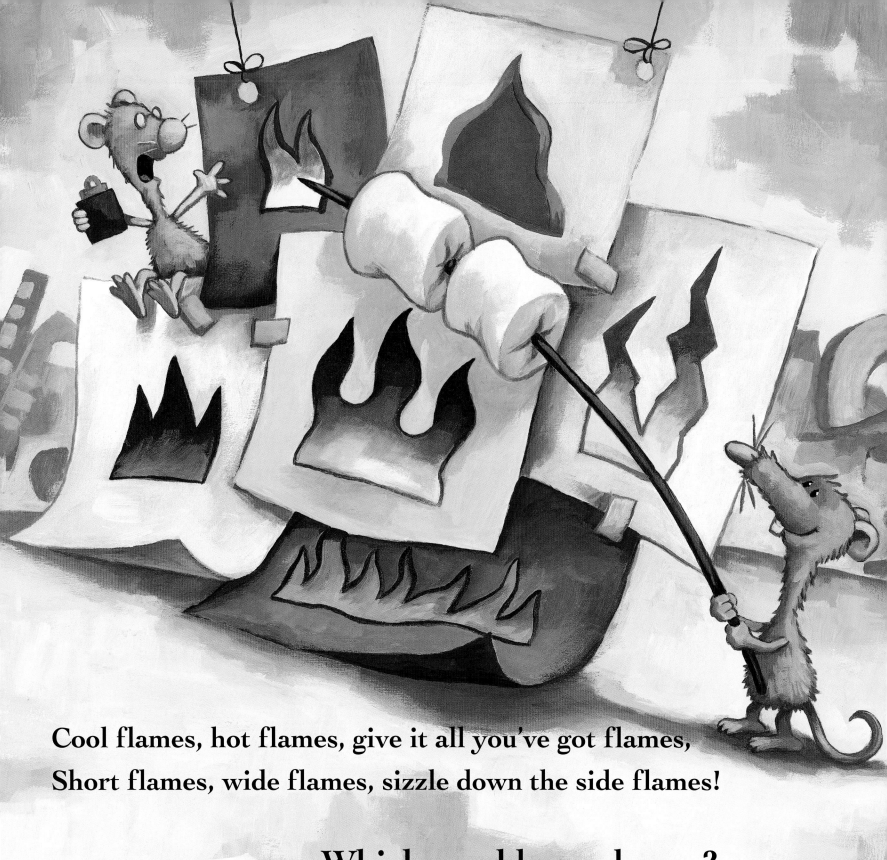

Cool flames, hot flames, give it all you've got flames,
Short flames, wide flames, sizzle down the side flames!

Which would *you* choose?

You'll get lost in our dust.

Stare face, scowl face, frowning grouchy-growl face,
Bored face, dare face, nose up in the air face.

Which would *you* choose?

Tough race, tight race, can't go left or right race,
"Oops!" race, "oh!" race, don't know where to go race!

Beep! Beep!

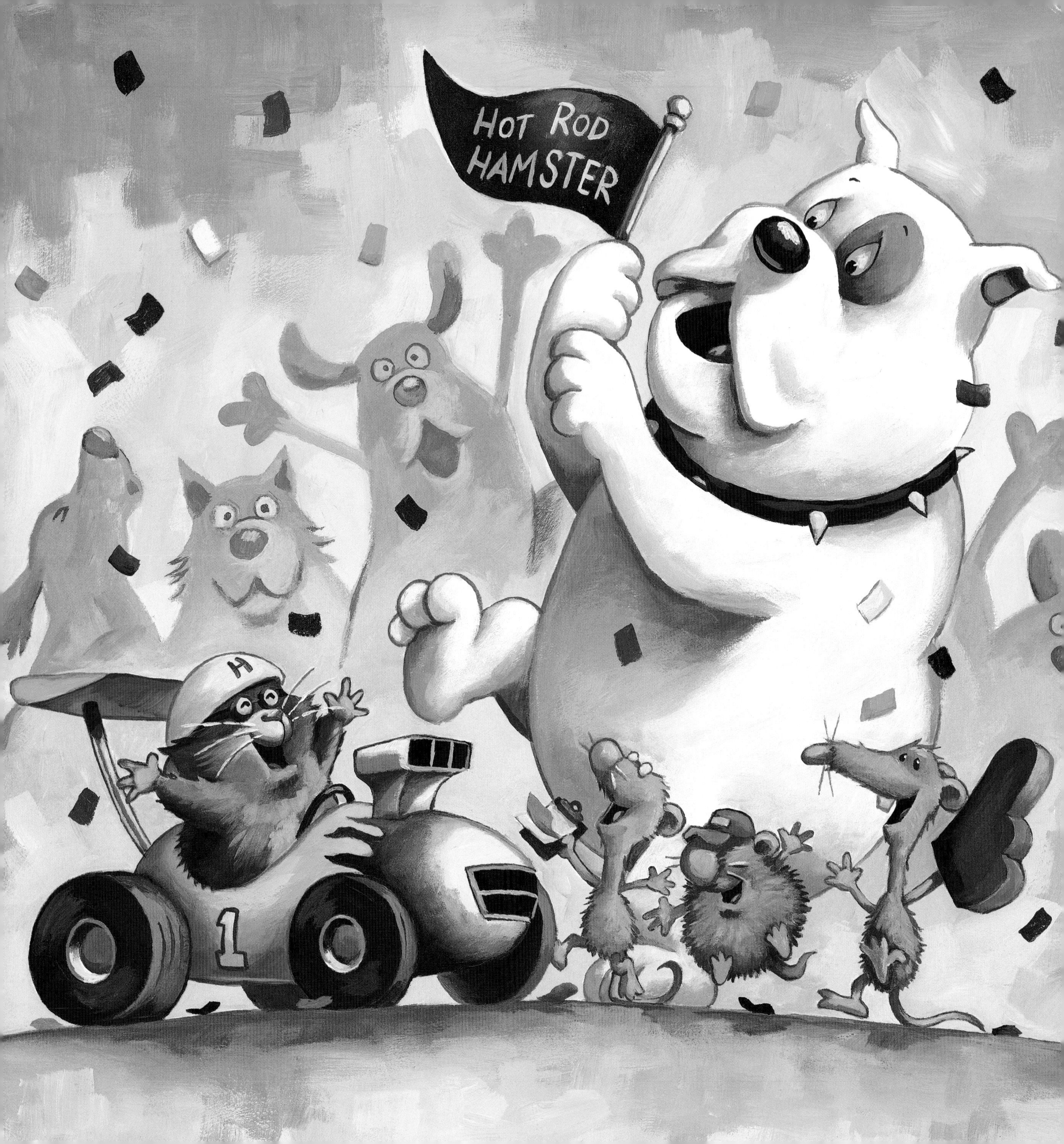
HOT ROD
HAMSTER

Crown prize, cup prize, cannot pick it up prize,
Silver prize, gold prize, lots of fun to hold prize.

Which would *you* choose?